www.carameltree.com

Not **All** Londoners Wear **Hats**

CARAMEL TREE

Chapter 1
Just Like a Londoner

Sun looked out of the train window. Big raindrops ran down the window.

"Can I buy a hat?" Sun asked.

"Of course, Sun." Mom was surprised. "What type of hat do you want?"

Sun showed his parents and his sister, Jin-Hee, a picture in his book about London. The picture showed a rainy day with people wearing hats and holding umbrellas.

"There are many famous places to see in London," said Sun. He turned the pages in his book. "Will we see Buckingham Palace?"

"Yes," replied Dad, "we must go there."

Sun really wanted to go to Buckingham Palace. He wanted to see the Royal Family.

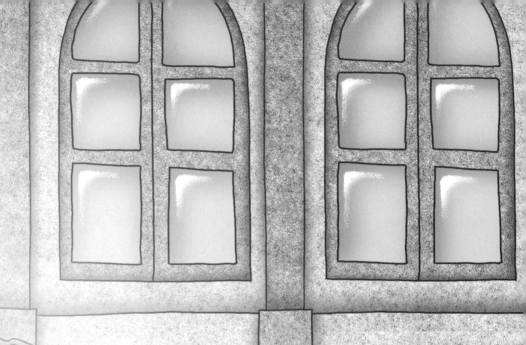

"Do you think the Queen drinks tea?" asked Sun. "My book says that English people like to drink tea."

"What do English people like to eat?" asked Jin-Hee.

"For breakfast they eat eggs and bacon. For lunch they eat fish and chips."

"Are you sure?" asked Mom.

"I read it in my book," said Sun.

"What else does your book say?" asked Jin-Hee.

"Real Londoners wear hats," Sun said. "Ladies wear big fancy hats. Men wear round black hats. Even kids wear hats." Sun wanted to get a hat so he could be just like a Londoner.

Jin-Hee decided she also wanted to buy a hat. Mom said they could all buy hats in London.

Chapter 2
Touring Around London

The next day, Sun and his family went on a bus tour.

"Great! It's a double-decker!" said Sun. "Let's go upstairs."

The bus started to move. It was not
easy to climb the stairs on a moving bus.
Jin-Hee nearly fell! Finally, they all climbed
the stairs and sat at the front of the bus.

The bus drove around all the famous buildings. The buildings looked just like they did in Sun's book. But one thing was different. Most of the people Sun saw were not wearing hats.

Sun was confused. His book showed Londoners wearing hats. *'Why aren't they wearing hats?'* Sun thought.

After the bus tour, the family went on
the London Underground.

"We must stay together," said Mom. "The
trains are crowded and it's easy to get lost."

When they got on the train, there were no empty seats. The family had to stand and hold on tight. The train went very fast. It was noisy and shaky.

At the next station, many people got off the train. Then, more people got on.

Sun kept looking for someone who was wearing a hat. No one was wearing a hat!

"There are lots of people in London, aren't there?" Sun asked.

Nobody answered him. Sun looked around. His family was gone!

Sun had been too busy looking for someone wearing a hat. He did not see when his parents got off the train.

Sun's heart was beating fast. What could he do? He was lost!

Chapter 3
Look for Someone in Uniform

Sun was alone in London. What should he do?

A man smiled and asked, "Are you okay?"

Sun wanted to be polite, but he didn't want to talk to a stranger. "I'm fine, thank you," he answered.

At the next station, Sun got off the train. He remembered what his parents had told him. *'If you ever get lost, look for someone in a uniform.'*

Sun saw a woman wearing a uniform.
She was selling tickets. She was wearing a
hat, but it was part of her uniform.

Sun walked over to her and said, "Excuse
me, I am lost. Can you help me, please?"

Soon after, Sun was sitting in a police car. It was his first time to sit in a police car. He told the policeman his name.

"Sun, that's a nice name. We need more sun in London." The policeman smiled.

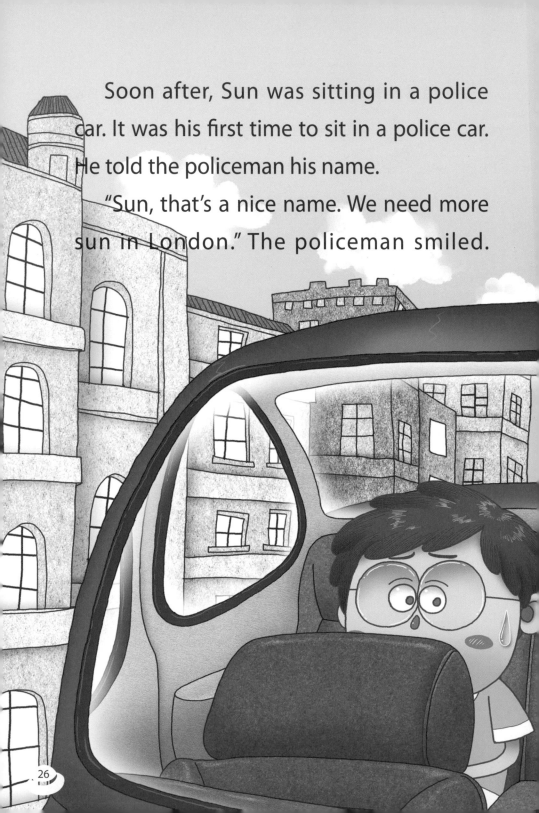

"Do you know the name of your hotel?" he asked.

Sun answered quietly, "No, I don't."

"Don't worry," the policeman said. "Your parents will call the police. Then I can take you to them."

It was lunchtime. The policeman asked Sun if he was hungry. Sun wasn't sure what to say. He said, "Yes, but I don't like fish and chips."

The policeman laughed.

Sun opened his book. "I read that English people eat fish and chips for lunch."

"This is a very old book, Sun," the policeman said. "Things have changed." The policeman pointed at a page, "Look at this picture. Not many people wear hats like those today.

Perhaps only the Queen does. The Queen likes to wear special hats."

Sun finally understood why he had not seen Londoners wearing hats.

"And we don't only eat fish and chips, you know," said the policeman. "In fact, I love Korean food."

Sun was surprised. "You like Korean food?"

"There's a Korean restaurant next to the police station. They make the best kimchee in London! Let's go there," said the policeman.

After lunch, the policeman received a call on his radio. Sun's parents were waiting for him at the hotel. The policeman let Sun speak on the radio with his parents.

It was fun. The best part was knowing he would see his parents again soon.

Chapter 5
The Palace

"We were so worried," Mom said. "What did you do?"

Sun told his parents everything.

"I also tried on the policeman's hat," said Sun.

"His tall black hat?" asked Jin-Hee.

"Yes, but it was too big," Sun laughed. "It covered my eyes."

The next day, the family went touring again.

Mom, Jin-Hee and Sun stood next to two big black and gold gates.

"Smile!" called Dad, and he took a photo. "Buckingham Palace is very special, isn't it?" he said.

"And it has finally stopped raining!" sang Jin-Hee.

A shiny black car drove past them. Sun saw a white glove waving at him through the car window. "It's the Queen! It's the Queen!" he shouted. "It *must* be the Queen. She's wearing a big fancy hat!"

"Can we go and buy our hats now?" asked Jin-Hee.

"Sure," said Mom. "Ready, Sun?"

"I've decided I don't want one." Sun smiled. "Not all Londoners wear hats."